A Brief History
of the United States
for the Easily Offended

A Brief History
of the United States
for the Easily Offended

Compiled and Edited by

William C. Even

Media Hatchery
Orchard Park, NY

ISBN: 978-0-9971276-6-9 (Paperback Edition)

Library of Congress Control Number: 2020911072

Front cover painting:
Decl@ration of Independence
by John Trumbull (1818)

Printed and bound in the United States of America
First Printing 2020

Visit HistoryForTheEasilyOffended.com

Published by Media Hatchery
P. O. Box 554
Orchard Park, NY 14127

MediaHatchery.com

To
My beautiful, wonderful wife, Nadine

Contents

Chapter One

The Colonial Period
1630 - 1764

A Brief History of the United States for the Easily Offended

A Brief History of the United States for the Easily Offended

The Revolution
1765 - 1783

Chapter Three

The New Republic
1784 - 1815

Expansionism
1816 - 1830

Expansionism *1816 - 1830*

Sl@very, Civil W@r, and Reconstruction
1831 - 1875

.

A Second Industrial Revolution

1876 - 1913

World W@r I
1914 - 1918

Prohibition,
The Roaring Twenties, and
the Great Depression
1919 - 1932

Chapter Nine

The New Deal
1933 - 1938

Chapter Ten

World W@r II
1939 - 1945

Post-W@r Era
1946 - 1959

Vietn@m Era

1960 - 1980

Reagan - Bush - Clinton
1981 - 2000

The New Century
2001 - 2019

Chapter Fifteen

The Apocalypse
2020

.

www.ingramcontent.com/pod-product-compliance
Lightning Source LLC
Chambersburg PA
CBHW071013120726
47910CB00004B/1499